# Stealing Home

*a novel*

*by*

SHAWN DURKIN

H·I·P Books

HIP Sr.

LIBRARY AND ARCHIVES CANADA CATALOGUING IN PUBLICATION

Durkin, Shawn, 1971–
    Stealing home / Shawn Durkin.

(HIP sr)
ISBN 978-1-897039-24-3

I. Title.  II. Series.

PS8607.U756S74 2007     jC813'.6     C2007-901267-1

General editor: Paul Kropp
Text design: Laura Brady
Illustrations drawn by: Catherine Doherty
Cover design: Robert Corrigan

1 2 3 4 5 6 7     07 08 09 10 11

Printed and bound in Canada

High Interest Publishing acknowledges the financial support of the
Government of Canada through the Book Publishing Industry
Development Program (BPIDP) for our publishing activities.

*Josh is just trying to fit in with the guys, trying to make his way at a new school. Baseball is the one thing he does really well. But his best friend on the school team is leading him into dangerous territory.*

## CHAPTER 1

# Trying Out

Things were different in the city, that's for sure. Back in Hinton, the small town where Josh came from, things never got as busy as this. Or as big. Western High School was huge. Josh thought he had never seen so many people in one place before. There were more students here than all the people in Hinton, and Hinton wasn't *that* small.

A pile of kids rushed past him. Some were talking on their cell phones. Some were texting or bobbing their heads to music on their iPods. They seemed to be very dressed up for school, wearing cool clothes like movie stars.

Josh looked down at what he was wearing. His jeans were the wrong style. His old runners were dirty with mud and grease. His sweatshirt was plain and boring. Back in Hinton everyone dressed like this. Josh had never given it much thought. Now he felt like a hick, a nobody.

Starting up at a new school is always tough. Starting in April, when the kids all know each other, is even worse. Why did his mother have to take her new job now? Would it have been a huge problem to wait a few more months? Josh sighed and walked through the main doors of the school.

Josh spent the day trying to blend in, just listening and getting the feel of things. He really didn't have to worry, though. All the other kids moved around him like he wasn't even there. He felt like a ghost, like no one could see him, or be bothered to look at him.

After school Josh made his way to the gym. This was the one thing he had been looking forward to.

Josh knew there would be open tryouts for the baseball team. Back home, Josh had been the starting pitcher for Hinton High. He had done well, playing against other small town school teams. But Western had a great team. They had won the city championship the year before. Getting on a team like that wouldn't be easy.

Josh got dressed in the locker room, picked up his glove and headed for the diamond. Lots of kids were there already, tossing balls around to warm up. Josh didn't know any of them and felt dumb standing by himself. He felt better when the coach blew a whistle and called the players to home plate.

Josh did a double-take when he saw the coach. The guy was tall with broad shoulders and bright orange hair. That's when Josh remembered the coach's name.

"Hey," he said to a kid running in beside him. "Isn't that Red Steadman?"

"In the flesh," said the kid. "A bit more flesh than in his playing days though." Then the kid laughed.

"I still have the card from the year he led the majors in home runs," Josh said. But the kid was no longer listening. Maybe Josh looked up to their famous coach, but the other Western kids didn't seem to care.

The guys gathered around Coach Steadman. They listened closely as he explained the drills they would be going through. They knew that the coach would be watching them, looking for the kids who could really play.

Josh started feeling better as he went through the drills. He didn't drop any balls and was throwing well. But he noticed many of the other kids were as good as he was. There was a lot of talent here at Western, lots more than there was in Hinton.

After a while, Coach Steadman called for the guys interested in pitching to come over to the mound. Josh made his way over. The other guys, of course, all knew each other. Josh felt his mouth go dry and his muscles grow tight. This tryout was going to be harder than he expected.

The coach was standing down at home plate, a batting helmet on his head and a bat in his hands. "Okay, boys," he called. "One at a time, step up and we'll go through an at-bat. This is your best chance to show me what you've got. Don't think you've got to take it easy on the old man."

"Yeah, right," Josh heard one of the other kids mutter. "An old man who spent nine years in the majors."

"Ryan," called the coach to the kid who had spoken out. "Since you think I'm deaf, you're up first. Let's see if your fastball survived the winter."

The other boys moved aside as Ryan stepped up. The guy was a bit on the skinny side but he had broad shoulders. He nodded to a couple of the other players, and then grabbed a ball.

"Strike him out, Ryan," said the kid beside Josh.

Ryan looked back at them and smiled. "Three years in a row? That would be a record wouldn't it?"

"Kind of," said the kid. "Since nobody else has even done it once."

Ryan turned away and faced the coach at the plate. He focused, wound up and pitched. The ball whizzed through the air, right across the plate and into the catcher's glove. The coach hadn't bothered to swing.

Ryan smiled at him. "Strike one," he said.

The coach just nodded and tapped his bat, waiting for the next pitch.

The next pitch was even harder, the pop in the catcher's glove even louder. Again the coach didn't swing.

"Strike two," said Ryan. The coach nodded again.

Josh was impressed. Ryan had some serious stuff and was able to throw it for strikes. Maybe he could out-pitch the famous Red Steadman.

Ryan threw his third pitch down the middle, hoping for a quick strikeout. But that was just what the coach wanted. Coach Steadman turned his body, swinging the bat through the ball, driving it hard — straight back over their heads. The guys turned to watch it bouncing toward a distant fence.

"Good stuff, Ryan," said the coach. "But not good enough. Who's next?"

Josh watched as the rest of the boys took their turns. None of them threw as hard as Ryan, although most would have made the Hinton team. The coach was hitting balls all over the park. Nobody even looked close to getting him out. Finally Josh was the only one left.

"You're the new kid, aren't you?" called the coach. "What's your name?"

"Josh."

"Where are you from, Josh?"

"I played last year with Hinton, Mr. Steadman."

"Hinton? You're a long way from home, aren't you?"

Josh was getting a bit nervous as all the other boys listened in. "My mom and I . . . we moved here last week, sir."

The coach nodded "Okay, but cut out that 'sir' stuff. It's Coach or Red, take your pick."

"Yes, sir … I mean, Coach."

"Well, step up to the mound, country boy. Let's see what you've got."

The other kids laughed as Josh stepped up onto the mound. Maybe they were laughing at him, or at what the coach had said. Still, Josh turned red in the face. He wasn't ready for this, not for any of it.

*Get your brain clear,* Josh told himself. *Think about baseball, not those jerks out there.* So Josh thought about all the things his Uncle Dan had taught him about pitching. Dan had played in the minors for nearly ten years. He had even been called up to the majors once but got hurt in his first game and never got another chance. Josh thought back to what his uncle had said about pitching. How do you pitch to someone new, someone who didn't know your stuff? "You have the advantage," Dan had told him. "You know something he doesn't. Don't give that up right away."

So Josh brought his hand to his glove, his fingers turning the ball. He stepped, brought his arm back and pitched. The ball travelled toward the plate at medium pace. Josh saw the coach's eyes go wide as he reared back and swung. The coach planned on smashing it over the fence, just as he had done before.

But at the last moment, the ball dropped out of the air. It came in low and hard. The coach swung over it. Strike one.

"Nice sinker," Coach Steadman barked. Josh nodded to him.

Josh heard Dan's words in his head as he steadied himself for his next pitch. "Use the count, keep him off guard." Josh threw the same pitch again but aimed it outside the far corner of the plate. The ball tailed away from the coach who stepped toward it but didn't swing.

"Ball one," the coach said. Josh nodded again.

Setting himself for the third pitch, Josh knew this was the time to bring the heat. He reared back and threw as hard as he could, aiming for the middle of the plate. He saw the coach's eyes go wide again, but this time with surprise. Coach Steadman swung but was too late and the ball popped into the catcher's glove as loudly as any of Ryan's pitches.

Josh heard a low whistle behind him and turned

to see that the other guys were all watching closely. Josh tried not to smile as he turned back to the coach and caught the ball from the catcher.

The count was one ball, two strikes. Josh knew the coach would expect him to throw a strike, just like Ryan had done. But Josh had balls to spare and didn't have to throw anything he didn't want to. He had the advantage and he knew it.

Josh set himself in position. So far, all his pitches had been low. He could see the coach crouching, ready to pounce on his fastball again. "Don't give 'em what they want," Uncle Dan always said. "Give 'em a surprise." So Josh reared back and threw a fastball. This time it was high and inside.

Coach Steadman started his swing, but he was too late to pull his hands in to adjust for the height. A swing and a miss. The ball popped into the catcher's glove for the third strike.

Josh heard a whoop behind him from the other kids, a sound that was soon silenced by a look from the coach.

"Good stuff, Josh," Coach said. "I think this team could use some of what you've got."

## CHAPTER 2

# High Five

Josh walked home alone after the tryouts. He made his way down busy streets lined with grey apartment blocks. His joy at striking out Red Steadman soon faded. As he walked past garbage bins and guys panhandling, Josh kept wishing that he was back home in Hinton.

Of course it wasn't his choice to be here in the city. It was his mother who wanted a new start. She was the one who wanted to make something of her life.

As far as Josh was concerned, they already had a perfectly good life. Josh and his mom had lived with his grandparents ever since his dad left, years ago. The big old farmhouse was the only home Josh had ever known.

But his mother wanted to move on. "You'll understand one day," she told him as they were driving out of town, their old car filled with boxes. "When you're grown up, living with your parents can be a real drag."

Her new job was in an office downtown, so she and Josh had moved into an apartment close by. Fine for her, lousy for Josh. He had been moping around the apartment, playing video games, ever since.

When he got home, Josh found his mother sitting on the sofa. She was watching the early news on TV.

"Ah, Josh," she said in a tired voice. "How was your first day?"

"It was okay, I guess," he replied. "The tryout went well." Then he paused before telling her. "I struck out the coach."

She smiled. "Way to go, Champ. Come here and get a hug."

Josh came over to the couch and put his arms around his mom. He hugged her for a moment, thinking how thin she was now. The city wasn't good for either of them.

Josh let go and walked into the tiny kitchen.

His mom looked up at him. "Okay," she said. "What's wrong?"

Josh shrugged. "I don't know. Nothing."

"Don't pretend, Josh," his mom said. "I can tell when something's wrong. You might as well tell me so I don't have to pick it out of you."

Josh sighed. His mom was like that. It was as if she could read his mind, or at least read his moods. "Okay, here's the truth. It was all weird today. I kind of felt like I didn't fit in. Everyone there had nice clothes and looked really cool, you know? It's not like Hinton. These kids have money. They've got … style. I mean, I felt like a hick."

She sighed. "I know what you mean. You need some decent clothes now."

"Does that mean we can do some shopping?" he

asked hopefully. "I really need some new stuff."

"Soon, Josh," she told him. "I had to put down a deposit on this place, then buy furniture and food. We just don't have that much money. Let me get paid a few more times and I promise to take you shopping."

"Yeah," he said. "Right."

"You'll understand, Josh. When you're older."

Josh sighed again. He heard that line before – for a good 16 years now.

"Look," his mom said. "Have you thought about getting a part-time job? I was your age when I got my first job, you know."

He thought about it for a second. "Actually," he said, "that's not a bad idea. And I might meet somebody cool. You never know."

"You never know," his mom agreed.

\*   \*   \*

At school, the tryout results were posted outside the gym. Josh saw his name with "outfield/relief pitcher" written beside it. He wanted to shout, but that wouldn't have been cool. So he smiled to himself and did a mental high-five. He had made the team!

Turning away from the board, he ran right into Ryan.

"Oh," he said. "Sorry."

"It's okay, man," Ryan replied. "No worries." Ryan looked at the board and smiled. "I see you made the team. Good to have you. By the way, I'm Ryan." He put out his hand to shake.

Josh took it. "Josh," he replied. "And you're a great pitcher, Ryan. That fastball is a killer."

Ryan laughed. "But you were priceless, Country. Striking out the coach like that. I'll never forget the look on Steadman's face."

"I guess I won't either."

Ryan shook his head. "Anyway, with you and me pitching, one more city title should be a breeze."

Josh couldn't help but smile. "I hope so," he said. His eyes wandered over to another part of the board. There was a heading that said "Part Time Jobs."

Ryan saw where he was looking. "Hey, Country,"

he said. "You looking for some work?"

Josh nodded. It was the second time Ryan had used the nickname. Josh wasn't sure he liked it but decided to say nothing. "Yeah, actually I am."

"I work at a grocery store. It's not much, just stocking shelves a couple of days a week after school. But the money is good. And my boss, Mr. Fujita, is a big baseball fan. I could put in a good word for you."

"Would you?" Josh asked. Then he felt stupid, as if he were begging for a job. That wasn't cool. Maybe Josh would never be really cool, but he didn't want to seem like a total loser. "I mean, thanks."

Ryan nodded. "No sweat," he said. "Drop by the store on your way home today. Sunshine Groceries on Fourth. Gotta run now, but I'll catch you later. See you, Country."

"See you." Josh's jaw was still open as Ryan walked away. *Country*, Josh said to himself, *what kind of nickname is that?*

Sunshine Groceries was just a block out of Josh's way on his walk home. The store wasn't very busy, with only a few customers slowly browsing the aisles. Josh walked up to the cash register. There was an older Japanese man with glasses and thin white hair adding up figures from a strip of paper.

"Excuse me," said Josh. "Are you Mr. Fujita?"

The man looked up. "Yes. Can I help you?"

Josh suddenly had a hard time finding words. "Um, my name is Josh. And I'm … uh, looking for some work … and Ryan said you might have something." Josh stopped talking. He sounded stupid and felt stupid.

But Mr. Fujita smiled at him. "So you're Josh?" he said. "Ryan talked about you. Have you got any experience?"

"Not a real job," Josh said. "But I used to help out a lot on my grandparents' farm. I'm a real hard worker."

"Oh, are you now?" the man said, still smiling. "I'm not sure if I really need someone … "

Just then someone came out from a storeroom at the back. "Hey, Mr. Fujita," the guy called. "Where do you want these … oh, hey, Josh."

Josh nodded.

Ryan turned to Mr. Fujita. "This is the guy I was talking about. Did he tell you how he struck out the coach yesterday?"

Mr. Fujita shook his head. "You struck out Red Steadman?" he said. "I hope he put you on the team anyway."

Ryan spoke up again. "He sure did, Mr. Fujita. Josh has got a great curve ball, and some serious heat too."

Mr. Fujita chuckled. "Well, good for you, Josh." The old man thought to himself for a second or two. "I tell you what. Fill out this form and bring it back tomorrow at four. You can work a shift and we'll see if you unpack boxes as well as you pitch a ball. If it works out, then the job is yours."

Josh did another mental high-five. Two in one day. Maybe moving to the city wasn't such a bad thing after all.

## CHAPTER 3

# Winning Streak

In their first game of the season, Western played Taylor High. It was an away game so that meant a bus trip across town. Coach Steadman came and sat beside Josh on the hard school bus seat.

"How are you doing, Josh?" he asked. By now the coach had dropped "Country," and Josh was glad about that.

"Just fine, Coach." Josh answered.

"Good," Coach said. "I just wanted to tell you

that Ryan will be starting today. You'll be on the bench, but if he gets tired I'll bring you in. You understand, don't you?"

"Sure," said Josh. "No problem."

Of course, it really was a problem. It felt strange for Josh to watch from the bench as his new team ran out on the field to play. Back in Hinton he had been the star. He had played every game. He had gotten all the cheers when he ran on the field. But at Western he was a nothing, and he'd better get used to it.

Ryan was pitching well that day. None of the Taylor batters came close to getting a hit off Ryan's fastball. Josh could have been sitting on the bench for the entire game.

But in the final inning, with the Western team leading 8-0, the coach called down the bench. "Hey Josh, grab a bat," he said. "You're up next."

"Me? Josh asked.

"Yeah, you," Coach Steadman told him. "Can't mess up a game at this point, can you?"

The other players laughed, but Josh got the message. He put on his helmet and made his way to

the on-deck area. He watched as the batter before him swung wildly at two pitches before slapping a single into left field. Now it was Josh's turn.

Then Josh stepped into the batter's box and got into his stance. He had been watching the Taylor High pitcher all day and knew the guy would try to throw a strike right away. But Josh was ready. He waved his bat and waited for the pitch. Again his Uncle Dan's voice came into his mind, this time talking about hitting. "Just keep it simple. Make contact. Swing right through the ball."

When the ball came toward Josh, it was just as he expected – a fastball right down the middle of the plate. Josh swung his bat. He heard the crack and felt the thump in his hands as he connected. Then he was off toward first base. He took several strides before looking up to see where he had hit the ball. It was a low hit heading toward the shortstop.

The Taylor shortstop fielded the hard ground ball, then turned and made the throw to second base. One man out. Their second baseman threw on to first before Josh could get his foot on the bag.

Double play.

Josh's first hit for the team – and he hit into a double play. *What a jerk*, Josh thought to himself. *Steadman will never let me play again.*

Josh found his glove and went to play left field for the final inning. He watched as Ryan struck out two batters. Then the last Taylor batter grounded out to first to end the game. 8-0: a sweet win for the rest of them. But Josh felt empty inside. He had done nothing for the win and had nothing to celebrate.

On the bus ride back, Ryan came over and sat beside him. "Hey, Country," he said with a smile. "Is that your winner's face? We're going to have to work on that."

Josh shook his head. "Sorry, man. You pitched a great game today. I'm just feeling a bit, I don't know, dumb. I mean, I hit right into a double play."

Ryan laughed. "That double play was the first one Taylor's pulled off in about twenty years. Those guys will be bragging about it for the next week. It was a good hit and they were lucky enough to catch it, that's all. And there was no harm done."

Josh tried to laugh, but it still felt hollow. "Yeah, right." He shrugged. "It's not just that play, though. I feel a bit out of place here. Things back in Hinton were easy. Here in the city, well, I just don't know."

"Aw, don't worry about it," said Ryan. "It just takes a bit of time to get used to things. Listen, I'm meeting a few guys at the mall, just to hang out. Why don't you hook up with us?"

Josh smiled. "Really?"

"Yeah, why not?" Ryan replied.

"Cool," Josh said. Then he smiled. Despite the double play, despite sitting out most of the game, he smiled.

At the mall, Josh spotted Ryan in the food court. He was standing at the center of a small group of

guys. "Hey, Josh," he called out. "Over here."

"Hey," Josh called out to Ryan.

Ryan's whole group turned toward Josh as he walked over. Josh felt like he was being checked over. Was he just a country hick, or would he fit in?

Ryan smiled and turned to the group. "Guys, this is Josh. Josh, this is Cam, Andrew and Tim. And you know Steve and Rohan from the team."

Josh nodded and tried to get the names straight in his head. Last week he knew no one in the city. Today he knew six guys. It was a start.

Josh and the guys hung around the food court

for a while. They talked about the game that day and a bunch of other things. Josh was quiet at first but soon joined in. Then the group walked through the mall, stopping in a few stores to check things out.

At one store, Josh noticed a tiny MP3 player. He had seen some of the other kids at school with it. Picking it up, he found the player was light and cool in his hand.

"Those things are amazing, don't you think?" Josh turned and found Ryan looking over his shoulder.

"I guess," he said. "I've never actually had one."

"Really?" said Ryan. "I've had mine for over a year. It's almost full of tunes."

Josh turned the tiny MP3 player over in his hand. "How do you get the music in there?" he asked.

Ryan laughed. "Country, you are really priceless. Hey, Cam, listen to this. . . . "

Once again, Josh felt stupid. He put the MP3 player down on the counter. Then he tried to laugh with the others.

Later on, the group split up. Ryan and Josh

ended up walking home together. Josh felt good after hanging out with the guys. Maybe he didn't belong here yet, but at least he knew a few people.

"Hey," he said to Ryan. "Thanks for this. It was good to get out of the house for a change."

"No sweat," said Ryan. "I moved here myself just a couple of years ago, so I know what it's like. Kind of a shock when you first come from a small town."

"Yeah, it's tough," Josh agreed.

"By the way, I got you a present for making the team." Ryan reached into his pocket and pulled out an MP3 player. It was the same one that Josh had been looking at in the store.

"Cool," said Josh. "I'll pay you back, like next payday."

Ryan shrugged. "Don't worry, man. Think of it as an early birthday present."

"My birthday was two months ago."

Ryan shrugged. "Okay, a late birthday present. It's nothing."

Josh shook his head as they walked on. Maybe it was nothing for Ryan, but it meant a lot to Josh. Maybe he finally had a friend in the city.

## CHAPTER 4

# Tastes Good Being Bad

After school the next day, Josh went to his shift at the grocery store. When he arrived, Ryan was already there. Ryan was unloading a box of drinks and stacking them on shelves.

For the next couple of hours, both Josh and Ryan worked hard. The two of them brought boxes out from the back and stacked shelves. Finally, Mr. Fujita told them to take a break. They walked together to the back of the store.

Looking over his shoulder, Ryan reached into his shirt and pulled out a drink. Josh saw right away that it was from the box they had just been unloading.

"Hey," he said. "Aren't we supposed to pay for that?"

Ryan laughed. "Oh, come on, Country," he said. "There are boxes and boxes of these. Nobody's going to miss one."

"Yeah," Josh said. "I guess. But back in Hinton, well, we didn't …"

"Oh, shut up," Ryan told him. "You're not in Hinton any more." Then he took another can from his shirt. "Here's your pop. Now drink it and forget about it."

Josh took the drink and looked at the can. Ryan was right, one or two cans of pop would never be missed. And besides, Josh was hot and thirsty from working. He opened it and took a drink.

Ryan laughed. "Tastes good being bad, doesn't it?" he said.

Josh shook his head and finished the rest of the drink. He threw the can in the recycle bin and went back into the store.

*Things are different in the city,* Josh told himself. *I just have to get used to it.*

The next day, Western was playing North Ridge High. Josh started the game in left field, batting fifth. He got his first on-base of the season in the third inning. But the next batter left him stranded, so he didn't score a run.

In the sixth inning, Ryan told Coach Steadman that he was getting tired. Western was trailing 2-1, so the game wasn't looking good. Still, it was Josh's big chance. Steadman called him in as the relief pitcher.

"Don't let them score again," said the coach as he flipped Josh the ball.

Josh did as he was told. It was still 2-1 when Josh came up to bat first in the next inning. He lined a base hit to right field as Ryan came to the plate.

Josh could see that he wanted to prove something. He looked very serious and focused. "C'mon Ryan!" Josh called from first base. "Hit one out of the park!"

The first pitch was a curve ball, outside, that Ryan let go. The next pitch was a fastball and Ryan swung hard. He connected with a loud crack. Josh watched as the ball flew high in the air, out over the outfielders' heads. It kept sailing over the fence for a home run.

"Just ask and you shall receive," Ryan laughed as the two of them ran home.

Western had a one-run lead, and Josh had three innings to pitch. He got through the first two just fine. But in the ninth, the Western third baseman dropped an easy ball. That gave the North Ridge team a runner on first.

Josh waited for the next batter. He knew what he needed for this guy, and he had a good idea of how to get it. His first pitch was low and inside, a ball, and the batter watched it go by. The next pitch was a little bit closer to the plate, still a ball, and the batter let it go by.

Josh could hear his Uncle Dan again. "It's like fishing," he'd say. "You just have to tease it closer and closer until it can't resist." He threw the next pitch just a tiny bit closer but also a bit lower. The batter hit the top of the ball, driving it down and taking away the power of the swing. The result was an easy ground ball to the shortstop, who stepped on second for one out, and then threw to first for a second. Double play and game over.

Josh had pitched his first win – and it felt fantastic!

\* \* \*

When he got in from practice the next day, his mother still wasn't home. He took a quick shower and got dressed. Ryan had asked him to come down to the mall to hang out with some of the guys, and that seemed like a good plan to Josh. But before he could leave, his mother came through the door carrying a large paper sack.

"Hi, Josh," she said. "Sorry I'm late. I had to get a report finished. I brought home some Chinese food for us." Then she stopped. She looked up and saw Josh standing there holding his jacket. "Were you going somewhere?"

"Um, yeah," he answered. "I'm meeting Ryan and a few of the guys at the mall."

"Well, you can sit down and have dinner before you go. Get down some plates."

"Actually," he said, "I'm not really that hungry. I'll grab something at the food court."

His mother stared at him. She seemed to be looking closely at his face. After a few seconds, she sighed. "Josh, I spent good money on this food," she said. "We can't let it go to waste."

"I'll have it for lunch tomorrow. Besides, I've got to get going," Josh told her.

She looked up at him. "Don't you have any homework?"

Josh shrugged. "A bit. I can finish it when I get back."

"And what time will that be?" his mom asked. "Last time you went to the mall, you didn't get back until way late. It was after I had gone to bed."

He shrugged again. "So?"

"So," she repeated. "So when do you get your homework done, Josh? I haven't seen you do any homework since we moved."

Josh turned red in the face. He didn't deserve this. He just wanted some time out with his friends. "My work will get done when it gets done. What's the big deal? I'm going out with some friends. Don't you want me to have any friends?"

His mom put some food down on the counter. "Actually, Josh, I wanted to talk to you. I had a call from the school today, from your math teacher."

Josh shrugged. "So what? Math sucks."

His mother shook her head. "Well, maybe you'd start to like it better if you weren't spending all your time playing baseball."

"Meaning?"

"Meaning this – maybe you should drop baseball."

His mom looked hard at him. She was serious.

Josh froze. "You wouldn't make me do that."

"Don't push me, Josh. You were a good student back in Hinton. Suddenly you come here and everything changes."

"Well, whose idea was that?" shouted Josh. "Whose idea was all of this?" He waved his arms around their new house. "I was plenty happy in Hinton … but you wanted to up and move to the city. You're the one who brought us here."

"Josh …"

"I've got my own life, you know. Sorry if it's not what you want, but it's *my* life." With that, Josh stormed out of the apartment.

Josh walked to the mall in the growing darkness, the wind cooling his hot face. He and his mother had arguments now and then, but this was different. She had no idea what he was going through. She thought he was still some kid to be dragged along wherever she went. So what if he didn't get his homework done? Josh had a job, he was playing ball and he was making some new friends. How could she expect more than that?

## CHAPTER 5

# A Bad Taste

It was a tight game against Barnard. The Western team was up by only one run. Watching from the outfield, Josh thought Ryan had things under control. Josh was surprised when the coach asked him to pitch the last inning.

"I think Ryan's just tiring out," said the coach. "You're fresh. You can come in and finish them off."

Josh looked over at Ryan before he said a word.

Ryan nodded at him. "Show them your stuff, Country."

Josh was nervous when he walked out to the plate. He was still upset about the fight with his mother. His mind wasn't really on pitching this game. It was on lots of stuff, here and at home and back at Hinton. Josh just wanted to throw hard and get the game over with.

His first pitch was good, but not good enough. The batter got lucky and blooped a hit into shallow center field.

Josh was angry about giving up the hit. He made up his mind to throw even harder to the next batter. That's what he threw – hard and fast. His first two pitches went right over the middle and popped into the catcher's glove. One more solid pitch and the game would be over. Josh smiled to himself. Then he reared back and threw as hard as he could.

It was one more down the middle. But this time the batter was ready.

Josh could tell it was bad news by the sound of the ball hitting the bat. From the cheering of the

crowd, Josh knew it was a home run. The man on first ran in, then the batter. Western had lost their first game of the season, 2-1. And it was all Josh's fault.

The bus ride back to school was quiet. Josh sat by himself in the back, his head propped against the window. He felt someone sit down beside him. When he looked up, Josh was surprised to see the coach.

"Tough game," said the coach.

Josh shrugged. "Yeah," he replied. "I guess."

"Well, it's part of the game," Coach Steadman went on. "Happens at every level. Even back when I was in the pros, I saw it happen to some really great pitchers."

"I know," Josh sigh. "Thanks, Coach. But it doesn't make me feel much better."

The coach sighed. "No, I guess not," Steadman told him. "You should think about it, though. Try to think about what you were doing that was different."

Josh looked up. "What do you mean?"

The coach stared at him. "Well, it looked to me

like you were throwing fastballs as hard as you could. You have a good arm, Josh, and a good fastball. But to be a great pitcher, you have to use your brain as well." He waited a few seconds for his words to sink in. "Anyone can throw hard, Josh. If you really want to be a success in this game, you have to throw smart. Do you know what I mean?"

Josh nodded. "I think so."

"I thought so, too," said the coach. "When you struck me out at the trial, you were pitching smart. Someone taught you pretty well, but today you forgot all that."

Josh looked down. "Yeah," he said. "I guess I did."

The coach smiled. "We all make mistakes, Josh. What matters is whether we learn from them. You'll get another chance, boy. But not two more chances, if you get my drift."

Josh looked up at him. "Yeah, I got it," he said. "Thanks, Coach."

Those words kept ringing through Josh's head. *But not two more chances, if you get my drift.* Josh had screwed up. He'd lost the game for Western.

Now the coach would give him one more chance, but not two. And his mother might not even give him one.

Josh and Ryan had to hurry to get to work on time. Mr. Fujita was standing near the cash registers when they arrived.

"Hi, boys," he said. "How was the Barnard game? Another big win for Western?"

Ryan looked over at Josh. "Not quite, Mr. Fujita. We lost a close one."

"Oh," said their boss. "That's too bad. You'll get them next time, I'm sure."

"Yeah, next time," they both said. But Josh was starting to wonder if he'd last until the next time. Maybe, just maybe, this was it.

Both boys began to work in the canned goods section. Stacking cans was heavy work and they both liked to get it done early. After that, they moved on to frozen foods. They were stacking frozen peas when Mr. Fujita came by.

"Boys I'm going to take a half-hour break. If you need me for anything, I'll be in my office."

"Sure," said Ryan. "We'll be fine."

As soon as Mr. Fujita left, Ryan pulled out his cell phone and punched in a number. "It's on," he said when someone answered. "See you in five."

"What's on?" Josh asked.

"Don't worry, Country," Ryan said. "Nothing that concerns you."

Five minutes later, Ryan said he needed to use the toilet. He headed for the back of the store … but he didn't come back.

Josh wondered what was going on. First the phone call, and now Ryan was gone. What was going on?

Making sure he couldn't be seen, Josh went to the back of the store. He looked up and down the last aisle. It was empty and there were only a few people up near the front of the store. At first he didn't see anything, but then he noticed that the back door was open. Most of the time, it stayed locked.

Then Josh saw the shadow of a man. Josh couldn't see who it was because the light was behind him, but he knew this meant trouble. Josh saw Ryan carry a large box over to the door. Ryan handed the box to the man.

Josh couldn't believe what he saw. Part of his mind came up with good reasons why Ryan might be passing a box out the back door. But the reasons didn't make sense.

At last, the man gave Ryan something that looked like a wad of cash. Ryan nodded, the man smiled and left. Then Ryan shut and locked the door behind him.

Suddenly Josh thought of the MP3 player Ryan had given him. It had never occurred to him that

Ryan might have stolen it. But now it made sense. Josh had wanted to be friends so badly it had made him blind to what was going on. Even thinking of the drink Ryan had given him brought a bad taste to his mouth.

By the time Ryan got back to the front, Josh was putting away the last of the peas. He wondered if he should say something. He wondered if he should tell Ryan what he saw. *But no,* he thought. *Better keep my mouth shut.*

"Took you long enough," Josh said instead. "I was about to send out a search party."

"It's not like you got much done while I was gone," Ryan laughed. "You need me here cracking the whip?"

Josh shrugged.

"Remember, I got you this job," Ryan told him. "I've got to make sure Mr. Fujita doesn't get ripped off by your being slack."

Josh just stared at him. The bad taste in his mouth just got worse.

# CHAPTER 6

# The Right Thing

Before their next game, Coach Steadman came over and tossed Josh the ball. "Ryan's got a sore elbow," he said. "I'm going to rest him today, so you're the man. Up for it?"

"You bet," Josh replied.

Josh felt a hand on his shoulder. It was Ryan. "Good luck, Country, just don't get used to it," he said as he walked to the bench. "You're not taking my job."

"Wouldn't dream of it," Josh said quietly.

Josh threw his best stuff that day. The other team's hitters couldn't get near him. When the umpire called strike three on the last batter, Josh's team ran out to the mound. They picked Josh up and carried him off the field on their shoulders. Western had won easily, 7-0.

But Josh was still troubled when he got to work. He had tossed and turned all night, trying to decide what to do. In the end, he decided to keep his mouth shut. Ryan was his friend, after all. Josh had seen *something*, but he wasn't sure what. Was it theft? And if it was, how could Josh prove it? And besides, it was none of Josh's business. Ryan had got him the job. How could he turn around and rat on his friend?

When Josh got to work, he slammed the front door coming in. It was Ryan who looked up. He had a strange look on his face. "Mr. Fujita wants to see you."

"Sure," Josh said. "No problem."

He made his way to Mr. Fujita's office. He wondered if Mr. Fujita had heard about the game.

Maybe he'd give Josh a bonus for great pitching. But when Josh reached the office, he saw that the old man wasn't smiling.

"Josh, please sit down."

Mr. Fujita looked at some papers on his desk, then at Josh. "I did a stock check last night, Josh. It made something very clear to me."

"What's that, sir?" Josh asked.

"Someone has been stealing from the store. We're missing boxes of stock from the back room,

Josh." Mr. Fujita waited, staring at him. "Do you know anything about it?"

Josh felt his stomach drop. Mr. Fujita knew! Ryan would be in real trouble now.

Josh thought fast. If he told Mr. Fujita what he'd seen, then the old man would wonder why he hadn't said anything. *Best to keep my mouth shut*, Josh told himself. Mr. Fujita will figure it out by himself.

"No," Josh told him. He tried to keep his face a blank.

Mr. Fujita straightened up. "Well, there's one thing I do know. All these thefts began when you started working here, Josh."

"But, sir …" Josh began. Then his mouth felt too dry to speak.

"I can't prove anything, Josh. But I know what I have to do." Mr. Fujita looked hard at Josh, then shook his head. "Clear out your locker and go home, Josh. I'm going to have to let you go."

Josh froze. He stared at Mr. Fujita as the words sank in. Josh didn't know what to say or do. He felt like someone had punched him in the stomach and knocked the wind out of him.

Ryan was waiting out near the front door when Josh came out. "What was that about?" he asked.

Josh turned to him, his eyes smarting. "It was about me losing my job."

"What?" asked Ryan. "Why?"

"I think you know why," replied Josh, anger starting to build in his voice. "Someone has been stealing from the store. And Mr. Fujita thinks it was me."

"You've got to be kidding."

"I wish I was," Josh told him. "But you know the truth, Ryan. The old man is blaming the wrong guy."

Ryan looked surprised. "Wha … what do you mean?"

"You know what I mean," Josh sighed. "And you know the right thing to do." With that, he turned and walked out of the store.

As he made his way through the city streets, Josh had to fight back tears. Just a few days ago everything had been going so well. He'd made some friends and found a job. He'd pitched the best

game of his life. He'd begun to think that moving here was a good idea.

But now he had nothing. His life tasted like ashes in his mouth. Josh knew there was only one person at fault. There was only one person who could clear his name. But would Ryan do the right thing?

# CHAPTER 7

# Fastball to the Shoulder

Then came the deep freeze. Ryan and Josh stopped speaking to each other. The silence was just fine as far as Josh was concerned. Ryan seemed to be avoiding him. He turned and walked the other way when he saw Josh coming down the hall. He left the lunchroom by the other exit when Josh walked in. They were like two strangers.

At practice on Thursday, the coach asked Josh to pitch for batting practice. Josh was glad to. He

McLean County Unit #5
201-EJHS

was throwing easily, just staying loose and giving hitters easy balls they could drive to the outfield.

Then Ryan came to the plate.

Josh felt all the anger surge up inside him. It all came back – the theft, the blame, the betrayal. He could feel the heat of anger in his neck. The muscles in his arms grew tense.

Josh wound up and pitched. It wasn't an easy ball like he'd thrown to the others. This pitch was hard and straight – aimed right at Ryan.

Ryan's eyes grew wide as he saw the ball coming at him. At the last minute, he turned and pulled back. Still, the ball hit him on the shoulder with a thud.

"Sh--" Ryan swore. "You did that on purpose!" he said, throwing down his bat. Then he came racing toward the mound. In no time, Josh and Ryan were face to face.

"I said, did you aim that on purpose, Country?" Ryan screamed.

"Maybe I did," said Josh. "Maybe you deserved it."

Just as they looked ready to fight, the coach

came running over. He quickly stepped between them. "Hey, cut it out, both of you."

"You saw that pitch," Ryan told the coach. "That was no accident."

Josh shrugged, then smiled. "I guess it slipped," he said. "Go on, Ryan, give me another try."

Instead, Ryan gave Josh a shove.

"I said that's enough!" shouted Coach Steadman. "Both of you, I want you running laps. Stay half a lap apart. And don't think I won't be watching you." He glared at both of them. "Now move it!"

Josh ran off first. He was glad the coach hadn't told him to say he was sorry. He'd rather run laps *all day* than do that.

When the practice was over, the coach called them over. The three of them stood around the bench.

"Either of you care to explain what that was about?" Coach Steadman asked.

Josh and Ryan were both silent.

The coach waited for a while, then shook his head. "I didn't think so. Stubborn as mules, both of you."

Still, the two were silent.

The coach clapped them both on the shoulder. "I thought you two were friends."

"Were," Josh snapped back. Maybe that one word explained it all.

The coach looked between them. "I don't know what's going on, but it's not going to affect the team." he said. "You're both suspended for the game tomorrow."

"But Coach…" said Ryan.

"That's not…" said Josh.

"If you want to sit out more games, you can keep talking."

Josh and Ryan both shut their mouths.

"That's what I thought," the coach told them. "And don't think this means you have tomorrow off. I expect to see you two in the stands, sitting together. Not fighting, just sitting."

Josh and Ryan looked at each other, surprised.

"That's all, now hit the showers."

The next day, Josh got to the diamond first. He found a seat several rows up, then sat down. A few minutes later, Ryan climbed up and sat down beside him.

They sat in silence for a few minutes. Both of them felt awkward. Neither wanted to be the first to speak.

At last, Josh broke the deadly silence. "So who's pitching?" he said.

"Perry," said Ryan.

"Are you kidding?" Josh replied. "He's going to get killed."

"Yep," Ryan agreed. "But it's not like there's a lot of choice, is there?"

They were silent again. *Was Ryan blaming him?* Josh wondered. This wasn't his fault. Josh wasn't the one who started it all.

It was a few minutes before Ryan spoke again. "You know I wasn't kidding yesterday. You really could have killed me."

Josh looked at his hands. "Yeah," he said. "I guess part of me wanted to. But I'm sorry, I guess. It was stupid."

Ryan rubbed his shoulder. "Well, I've got a heck of a bruise ... if that makes you feel any better."

Josh nodded. "A little." And then he smiled.

They watched the game in silence. Western was in trouble right from the start. After the first inning, the team was already down 3-0.

During the break, Ryan turned to Josh. "Okay," he said. "You've worn me down. What will it take to set things straight?"

Josh looked at him. The answer was simple. Ryan should have been able to figure it out himself. "Go to Mr. Fujita and tell the truth."

Ryan laughed. "Yeah, right."

Josh wasn't smiling.

"You're serious? I should come clean, lose my job, get the cops on me, get killed by my parents … all so you'll be my friend?" Ryan shook his head. "Get real."

"I kept my mouth shut," Josh told him.

"Good thing you did," Ryan told him. "What about that drink you had? Or that MP3 player you've got?"

Josh looked at Ryan for a long time, not saying a thing. Finally he stood up. Still looking at Ryan, he pulled the MP3 player out of his pocket. He dropped it on the bench beside Ryan like it was a dead rat.

# CHAPTER 8

# A Little Justice

Without Ryan or Josh up on the mound, Western lost the game. Perry gave up fifteen runs. Even with the Western batters scoring ten runs, it had been one of their worst defeats ever. The loss dropped Western to second place going into the final round. Even worse, it showed the other teams that Western could be beaten. The former champs might not even make it to the finals.

The team was up against Grace Hill, their biggest rival. Grace Hill hadn't lost a game all season. They already had a spot in next week's city final. Western had to win to be able to play.

The rest of the team were glad to have Ryan and Josh back in the line-up. Today, Ryan was the starting pitcher. Josh took his spot in the outfield. All the players knew just how much this game mattered. A win gave them a chance at first place. A loss gave them a lousy third- or fourth-place finish. Even Ryan and Josh had to put aside their problems. This game was all that mattered.

In the second inning, Josh singled and stole second. Ryan came to bat with two outs.

Josh clapped from second base. "Come on, Ryan. Bring me home," he called.

Ryan shot him a look, but Josh couldn't figure out what it meant.

The next pitch was right down the middle. Ryan made contact, pushing a single into right field.

Josh was off like a shot. He went around third and set his eyes on home plate. With every step, he tried to will it closer.

Out of the corner of his eye, he saw the throw coming in. Josh dove head first, off to the left to avoid the catcher's tag. At the last second, Josh reached out with his left hand and touched the plate.

He was safe! 1-0 Western.

As the game went on, that one run became more and more important. It was still 1-0 in the fifth inning. That's when Ryan walked a batter who then went to second on a ground ball out. The next batter hit a bouncing ball out to Josh.

Josh ran at the ball. He could see the runner going around third and heading for home. Without breaking his stride, Josh caught the ball and launched a throw with all his strength. The ball flew straight into the catcher's glove a full second before the runner reached the plate.

By the eighth inning, the score was still 1-0. The coach came over to where Josh was sitting on the bench. "Ryan's getting tired," he said. "You're in for the ninth."

Josh just nodded. When the final Western batter was out, he jogged over to the mound. He felt a pat on the back just as he was about to step up. It was Ryan. "Three up, three down," Ryan said.

"No problem." Josh replied.

Ryan smiled. "Better not be, Country." Ryan looked like he wanted to say more but just turned and ran to the outfield.

Josh was facing the top of the line-up for Grace Hill – the best hitters on their team. Still, he felt relaxed. He knew that they wouldn't touch the ball if he just pitched smart.

And Josh was smart. He kept mixing up his

pitches and changing speeds to keep the batters off guard. The Grace Hill batters couldn't get close. With a final pop, his last pitch hit the catcher's glove. The game was over. A 1-0 victory. Maybe not a great win, but good enough to get Western into the finals.

As the team ran out to the mound, Josh held his arms in the air and let out a whoop. He'd done it! He'd struck out Grace Hill on nine pitches. Three up, three down.

*　*　*

That Saturday, Josh was at home when the doorbell rang. He looked over at his mother who was reading a book on the sofa. "Expecting someone?" he asked.

She didn't even look up from her book. "I'm not the one with the social life, remember?"

"Oh yeah," he said, heading for the door.

When Josh opened it, he was surprised to see two policemen standing there. "Hello," he said, a bit nervously. "Can I help you?"

The policemen introduced themselves and asked if he was Josh. This brought his mother to the door. In no time, the police were talking to both of them.

"Josh," said the first cop, "we're here because someone has been caught stealing from the store where you used to work. The owner told us that he had suspected you. We just wanted to check if you had any more information for us."

"Do you know who did it?" Josh replied.

The policeman kept a poker face. "I really can't reveal the suspect's name. But he was caught red-handed, so you might have some idea who it was."

Josh said nothing. A million thoughts ran through his mind, but he kept his mouth shut.

"You worked at the store, Josh. Did you ever see anyone take anything? Did anyone put something aside he could pick up later?"

Josh *had* seen that. He *could* tell the cops what he knew. But Josh just shook his head. "No, sorry. Nothing like that."

"Okay," replied the policeman. The two cops turned to go. "If something comes to mind, here's my card. Just call, no one has to know."

"Thanks," Josh said.

"And by the way, Mr. Fujita would like to see you," the cop added. "Looks like he made a big mistake. Maybe he's got something to say about it."

The grin on Josh's face wouldn't quit. He was still smiling when he got to the store. Mr. Fujita was standing near the checkout.

"Ah, Josh," Mr. Fujita began. He seemed a little

awkward. "I'm glad you came. Please come into the office."

Josh walked with him past rows of groceries. He felt good being back here, but he wasn't sure what would happen next.

"Josh," Mr. Fujita said, plopping down in a chair, "I owe you an apology. I was wrong to fire you without any proof. I just couldn't believe that Ryan was a thief. He worked for me for a long time and he always seemed like such a good kid."

Josh shrugged. Now he was the one who felt awkward. "Um, that's okay, I guess."

Mr. Fujita smiled. "But you really are a good kid, Josh. I'd like it if you could come back and work for me. I'll give you a raise. And just to say I'm sorry, please take these." He quickly handed Josh an envelope.

Josh opened the envelope and found two brightly colored tickets.

"They're for tomorrow's Hawks game," said Mr. Fujita. "I thought it would be a good idea for you to look at the diamond before the final. If you can't make it, I can exchange them."

"No, no," said Josh. "Tomorrow is fine." He kept looking down at the tickets in his hands. He had never been to a major league game before, and the Hawks were leaders in their division. Now he held two Hawks tickets in his hands. "I don't know what to say, Mr. Fujita."

Mr. Fujita laughed. "Say you'll start work on Tuesday."

Josh grinned back. "I'll start work on Tuesday."

# CHAPTER 9

# Hey, Champ

Josh and his mother arrived at the stadium early. He held the tickets in his hand, a bit dazed by all the noise and people. The stadium was filled with screaming fans. There were all sorts of video screens and flashing lights.

"It's like being inside a pinball machine," Josh said to his mom.

It turned out to be their best day since coming to the city. They ate hot dogs, did the wave, and cheered until they lost their voices. Josh was blown away by how good the major league players were. The pitchers seemed to throw much harder than they did on TV. The fielders could catch any ball that came close. They worked as a team, a real team, the way Steadman always talked about it.

Josh tried to picture himself out on the mound with all these people watching. Then he shook his head and thought again. He wouldn't be pitching the final, Ryan would. It wouldn't be his game, it would be Ryan's.

Josh looked out to left field, where he most likely would be playing. There seemed to be a lot of room out there. The whole field looked so much bigger than the school fields he had always played on. The finals would be Josh's first try at the big time – and he was scared.

"Thinking about the finals?" his mom asked.

"How did you know?"

"I'm your mother," she told him. "I'm supposed to know."

In the end the Hawks won 5-4. They scored three runs in an exciting ninth inning to put it away. The perfect end to a perfect day.

Just before the city final, Coach Steadman put the team through an intense workout. All the players were working hard. They were pushing themselves to be as sharp as possible the next day. They were all excited about playing at the city's main stadium. They were looking good, all of them. All of them except Ryan – who wasn't there.

Josh hadn't seen Ryan since the day the police had come to his door. Ryan hadn't been to school and, of course, he hadn't been to work. None of his friends seemed to know what had happened, and Josh wasn't going to be the one who told them.

After the practice, coach Steadman called the team together. He looked a bit nervous as the group of sweaty boys gathered around him. "Boys," he began, "we've had a great season. Tomorrow we'll be going for the championship for the second year in a row. We've come a long way. There are a lot of young men in this city who'll never play in a championship game. To get there twice in a row is a very special thing. And I wanted to tell you just how proud I am."

He paused for a moment and looked at the players.

Then he went on. "I have some news about the line-up to pass on. No doubt you've seen that Ryan isn't here today." He paused again, looking at the ground, then back up at them. "Earlier this week, Ryan was suspended from the team."

The team seemed to cry out in surprise all at once, but the coach kept going.

"I'm not going to say what happened because

that is a private matter. I know many of you are his friends. If he wants to tell you, that's up to him. All I can say is that Ryan won't be playing for us tomorrow. Josh will be starting the game. I know he'll pitch us to the title."

Josh was amazed. He wasn't the only one. The rest of the team looked shocked, and most eyes turned toward him. Josh looked down and scuffed his feet before raising his eyes to meet their stares.

Josh was still lost in thought when he pushed open the door to his apartment. He was halfway to his room before he even noticed that there was someone else sitting with his mom in the living room. It wasn't until he heard a voice that he stopped.

"Wow," the voice said. "I've never seen Josh that focused before. What have you been doing to the kid?"

"Uncle Dan!" Josh cried out. "What are you doing here?" He stepped forward and gave his uncle a hug.

Dan slapped him on the back and laughed. "Are you kidding? Do you really think I'd miss my nephew playing in the city final?" He smiled at Josh. "Even if he is playing left field."

"Well, I won't be," said Josh. "I'm starting."

Both Dan and his mother were surprised, so Josh told them what the coach had said. That led into telling Dan about what had happened at the store. And that led into a long talk about everything that had gone on since they came to the city. By the time the talk was finished, they had gone through two pizzas.

"Hey, Champ," said Dan. "You need a good night's sleep before the game. Get off to bed and I'll see you in the morning. I'll talk to you about the game on the way there."

## CHAPTER 10

# The Big Game

U ncle Dan and his mother wished Josh luck, then went heading off to find seats in the stands. There weren't as many people there as there had been for the Hawks game. Still, it looked like all the students from both schools were there. Western's fans were behind their dugout on the third-base side. Grace Hill's fans were behind theirs on the first-base side.

Josh followed his teammates into the dressing

room. He was amazed. The room was huge and filled with sofas, TVs and exercise equipment.

"Don't let the glitzy stuff go to your heads," the coach shouted. "Just get ready to play ball."

Still, it was hard to stay cool. The whole team was nervous when they ran out on the field to warm up. Tossing a ball back and forth, Josh looked up to see his face on the scoreboard four stories high. He was so surprised that the ball just missed hitting him in the head.

Before the game started, Coach Steadman called the team in for a talk.

"Okay, boys," he began. "Don't go nuts because we're in a pro stadium. Remember, it's just a baseball diamond like any other. You're going out there to play baseball. Just baseball. You're not to watch for your picture to come up on the big screen." The coach glanced at Josh. He must have been watching when Josh nearly got hit with the ball.

"This is it, boys. This is the big one. You'll remember this day for the rest of your lives. If we all work at it, we can make this game one fine memory. Now go get 'em."

The crowd roared as the Western players ran on to the field. Josh jogged slowly to the mound. Then he began his warm up.

*It's just another baseball diamond,* he told himself. Just like Uncle Dan had told him.

The first Grace Hill batter came to the plate. Josh threw a curve ball, but it came in low. Somehow the plate seemed farther away than before. Josh tried again, and this pitch was outside. Try as he might Josh just couldn't throw a strike. He walked the batter on four pitches.

Josh walked around the back of the mound, trying to calm his nerves. He looked into the crowd and saw his mother and Uncle Dan watching him. Dan gave him a thumbs up. Maybe it was a vote of confidence that he needed. Josh turned back to face the Grace Hill batter. *It's just another baseball diamond,* he told himself. And it was.

Josh's next pitch was a hard fastball right over the plate. He smiled to himself and kept focused. Two pitches later the Grace Hill batter was struck out. He threw down his bat in disgust.

Josh went right after the next batter. Soon he

had him down two strikes. He knew the batter would be expecting him to go for the kill. So Josh decided to surprise him. He'd waste a ball outside, then go for the strike out.

But from the moment he threw the ball, Josh knew it was a mistake. He felt the ball just slip off the end of his fingers. It went right down the middle rather than well outside, where Josh had planned. The batter turned on it, and his bat connected with a loud crack.

Josh watched over his shoulder as it flew away. The ball kept on sailing over the Western right fielder's head. Gone. A home run. Josh had given up a stupid home run.

Josh kept shaking his head as the two players circled the bases. First inning, and already Western was down 2-0.

Josh looked up at Dan in the stands. Dan gave him a shrug and called out. "Lots of game left, Josh!"

Josh nodded to him and looked over at Coach Steadman. The coach just gave him a shrug, not blaming Josh for what happened.

So Josh stepped back up to the mound. He got the next two players to ground out and then headed back to the dugout.

Josh wasn't the only player with a case of nerves. The Grace Hill pitcher seemed to have some trouble getting settled. Western scored a run in their half of the inning, as well. It wasn't enough to tie the game, but it helped.

Then both teams went into defensive mode. When Josh came to bat in the seventh inning, it was still 2-1.

The batter before Josh walked. He was standing on first, looking at Josh. Anything more than a single would bring him home with the tying run.

Just before he walked out to the plate, Josh heard someone call his name. It was Uncle Dan, beside the dugout. He was waving Josh over.

"Hey," Dan told him, "watch the pitcher's glove. He touches it to his knee when he throws the curve."

Josh nodded and headed out to the plate. He watched the first two pitches go past, one for a strike and one for a ball. The second pitch was a

curve. Just as Dan had said, the Grace Hill pitcher
rested his glove on his knee as he threw the ball.

*Okay, so I know the pitch,* Josh said to himself.
*Now I just have to hit it.*

Josh stepped out of the box to think for a second.
He glanced up at the Grace Hill crowd of fans.

He saw someone sitting way up above the other
fans – a guy wearing a cap pulled down low and
dark glasses. It was Ryan! The guy just couldn't
keep away from the final game.

Josh took another step back. He fixed his batting gloves to get a bit more time.

He thought about Ryan coming to the game. It was funny, but Josh didn't hate Ryan. Ryan had never forced Josh to be part of what he did. In truth, he had kept his stealing hidden from Josh. Ryan had made mistakes, sure, but he was paying for them. Maybe he was learning from them. Josh had no reason to be angry, not here, not now.

Josh looked up again, straight at Ryan, and gave him a smile. He saw Ryan give him a thumbs up, then he stepped back into the box. Josh focused on the pitcher. He knew what was coming, and he had to be ready.

As the pitcher threw the next pitch, Josh saw him put his hand on his knee. The ball looked like it was going to be just outside. But Josh knew better. Josh knew that it would drop and curve into the strike zone.

So Josh swung. He swung where he thought the ball was going to be. He swung blindly, but still the bat made good contact. The ball went sailing deep into the outfield.

By the time the fielder got to it and threw it back, Josh was standing at second base. The runner on first base had scored. It was 2-2.

Josh called time and called the coach over. Josh pretended that he had hurt his knee, but that was just for cover. When Steadman came over, Josh explained the glove to the knee signal. Then Josh got up and jogged back to second. He kept nodding his head to say that he was all right. Meanwhile the coach went to talk to the next batter. The message was passed on.

Josh watched as the next batter waited for the curve. The batter quickly slapped a single into right field. Josh ran hard around third and beat the throw from the outfield. Western was up, 3-2.

Looking up, Josh saw the Grace Hill coach come to the mound. He was changing pitchers. So much for the glove-to-knee signal. The new pitcher ended the inning with two quick outs.

Still, Western had the lead. They had the championship in their hands. But it was up to Josh to keep hold of it.

## CHAPTER 11

# Pitching for the Win

In the eighth inning, Josh faced the bottom three batters in the Grace Hill line-up. He got the first batter to ground out to second. Then he struck out the second batter before getting the third to hit a weak fly ball to third base. He jogged back to the Western dugout and sat down. In what seemed like a few seconds, the Grace Hill pitcher retired the side.

Josh was on his way back out again. The ninth

inning. It meant the championship if Josh could hold Grace Hill scoreless. It meant trouble if they scored a run. And it might be disgrace if Grace Hill scored two.

As he walked to the mound, Josh looked up above his team's dugout. His mom and uncle were sitting there. They were both smiling and cheering him on. Then he turned and looked to where Ryan had been sitting. His old friend, and sometimes enemy, was nervously rocking back and forth. Ryan must have known how Josh was feeling. He'd been there, on the mound, a year before. Now it was Josh's turn.

Josh was facing the top of the order once more. It was just like the week before – up by one run with the game on the line. Back then, it had been for a chance to play in the finals. Now it was for the championship.

Josh decided to start the first batter with a fastball. He threw fast and straight, but was taken by surprise when the batter turned and bunted the ball.

Josh raced in toward where the ball was rolling.

He grabbed it in one hand, turned and threw it to first. The throw was just in time.

Josh exchanged a nervous look with his catcher. One out, two to go.

Next up was the number-two hitter. Josh had struck him out four times in the last two games. He was pretty sure this guy couldn't hit his pitches. Again, he threw the fastball.

Then came the surprise. The batter swung and drove the first pitch hard down the left-field line. Before Josh could even look, a loud cheer went up from the Western fans. Josh turned to see the Western third baseman stretched out on the ground. He held the ball up in his glove.

Two outs.

At last came Grace Hill's power hitter, a guy named Marlin. He was the league leader in home runs. If Josh could get him out, the game would be over. Western would win the championship. But if Josh made a mistake, it could all go the other way. This guy could tie up the game with just one swing.

Marlin watched Josh's first pitch go by for a strike. Then he stepped back as the second pitch drifted inside. Ball one.

Josh thought he could get Marlin to swing at one outside, but he guessed wrong. Marlin's bat stayed on his shoulder as ball two was called by the umpire.

*Stay loose*, Josh told himself. *Walk him if you have to, but stay loose.*

Josh threw the next pitch low over the outside corner of the plate. He thought he'd thrown a strike but the umpire called ball three.

Josh walked around the back of the mound to

clear his mind. He knew he could walk the guy. He knew that the next batter wasn't as good. But if Marlin got on base, that might bring the winning run to the plate. Josh wanted to end this now. He punched his glove and got set once more.

He threw a fastball. He aimed it at the inside part of the plate. Even if Marlin got the hit, he couldn't extend his arms and use his power. Then, good luck. Marlin's swing was late. The ball popped into the catcher's glove for strike two.

The crowd was quiet in the stands. It was ninth inning, two out, full count. Everyone knew what that meant.

Josh could feel the sweat running down his forehead. He looked up at the stands again. Uncle Dan gave him a nod, but Josh had no idea what that meant. Josh looked over at Coach Steadman, but his face was set like steel.

Josh got set. Again, he wanted to end it with this pitch. He threw at the same spot but with a curveball this time. But Marlin was too good. The batter made a change at the last second, then fouled the ball away to the left.

Still full count. The tension in the stadium stayed high as Josh's next three pitches were hacked away for foul balls.

Josh tried everything he knew for a strike out. But Marlin was dug in, determined not to get out. He wasn't risking a big hit, but he wasn't risking a strike either.

Josh began to lose it. He wanted this batter out. He wanted this game to be over *now* – not later – but *now*. So Josh reared back with his next pitch. He threw it as hard as he could, right toward the middle of the plate.

Even before hearing the crack of the bat, Josh knew it was a mistake. He looked at the crowd as they watched the ball sail away, high over his head. Josh felt completely drained. He'd given that pitch all he had, and had let his whole team down.

But the Western outfield had not given up. The center fielder ran back toward the fence, watching the ball as it came toward him. At the last possible moment, he jumped against the fence. He reached up as high as he could. Then there was a split second that lasted forever.

Josh held his breath. The ball ended its arc to the fence. The center fielder seemed frozen in mid air … and then the ball plopped into his glove.

The Western fans exploded. The team ran to the mound to mob Josh. The right and left fielders lifted the center fielder on their shoulders.

It was the game, the championship, all that they wanted!

Josh felt himself raised above the team's heads. Everyone was dancing and cheering on the field. He looked into the crowd and saw his mother and Uncle Dan on their feet.

Then Josh looked over to where Ryan had been standing. He couldn't see him in the stands, but soon heard a voice calling to him from below.

"Hey, Country!" the voice called.

Josh looked down to see Ryan, then jumped down. Ryan grabbed him in a bear hug. "I knew you could do it!" he yelled.

Josh laughed. "That makes one of us," he said. "I'm glad you came."

"Yeah, well," said Ryan, "I couldn't miss it. And I owe you an apology, I think."

"Hey, there's plenty of time for that later," Josh told him. "Right now we've got some partying to do."

He put his arm around Ryan's shoulders. Together, they walked to where the league trophy gleamed in the sunlight.